W9-CIO-323

The artist wishes to thank Robert Copeland, Historical Consultant for Spode Ltd.,
Staffordshire, England, for his help with the note at the end of the book.

Published in the United States by North-South Books Inc., New York

Published simultaneously in Great Britain, Canada,
Australia and New Zealand by North-South Books,
an imprint of Nord-Süd Verlag AG, Gossau Zürich, Switzerland.

Library of Congress Cataloging-in-Publication Data
Drummond, Allan.
The willow pattern story / Allan Drummond.
Summary: The author retells a story heard as a child, one of many invented
to explain the landscape on willow pattern china, popular for the last 200 years.
In this, two young Chinese lovers are punished by one's cruel mandarin father.
ISBN 1-55858-171-5 (trade binding)
ISBN 1-55858-172-3 (library binding)
[1. China—Fiction. 2. Love—Fiction.] I. Title.
PZ7.3.D8247Wi 1992
[Fic]—dc20   91-46239

British Library Cataloguing in Publication Data
Drummond, Allan
Willow Pattern Story
I. Title
823 [J]
ISBN 1-55858-171-5

1 3 5 7 9 10 8 6 4 2
Printed in Belgium

The illustrations in this book were done in gouache and pencil on watercolor paper.
Stencils were used to create some decorative patterns.

The Willow Pattern Story

Allan Drummond

North-South Books

NEW YORK

*F*LY WITH ME, over China, and
down into the landscape of the willow pattern.
Come, smell the exotic scent of peonies and
camellias below the windows of the Great
Pagoda. Hear the sweet song of the birds in the
paradise garden, and the faint sound of waves
lapping against a little boat carried downriver
by the tide. See, under the weeping willow,
three figures hurrying across a bridge. And
high above, two mysterious love birds
forever kissing. . . .

In a pagoda, beside a weeping willow tree, an old Chinese mandarin lived with his beautiful daughter, Koong Shee.

The pagoda garden was surrounded on one side by a wide, deep river, and on the other by a zig-zag fence too high to climb.

This garden was Koong Shee's prison, for she was forbidden to leave it. Her father would say, "My child, I have promised your hand in marriage to the old merchant Ta Jin. Until that day you must hide your face from everyone but me."

So the birds became Koong Shee's only friends, and among the fantastic shapes of apple, orange and fir trees, and the scented petals of peonies and camellias, they called to her all day long, and came to her hand for food.

On a hill near the edge of the garden, in a little house overlooking the landscape, the mandarin's servant Chang worked at his desk. He managed all the old man's business, and cared for the plants and the trees. He, too, knew the birds by name, and they came to his window ledge for food.

It was spring, and before long, Koong Shee and Chang had fallen in love. But how had this happened? A pair of turtle doves knew their secret. The two birds began carrying messages for them —

written on tiny pieces of bamboo
paper — across the tree tops.

One morning Chang wrote, "As the
willow blossom falls onto the water, so
my heart flies to you. Meet me on the
banks of the river, as the tide turns
under the moon."

When night came, the
lovers finally met under the weeping
willow, hidden from the Great Pagoda
by an apple tree.

BUT AT THAT MOMENT the mandarin awoke, and going out into the moonlight, he saw his daughter in Chang's arms.

The mandarin's anger at finding his daughter with a poor servant was so great that he sent Chang away forever.

Then he told Koong Shee that she must forget Chang and marry the old merchant. This she would not do, so he ordered a house to be built, jutting out into the deep river, within sight of the Great Pagoda. Here he locked Koong Shee away.

A YEAR PASSED, and one day the mandarin took his friend the old merchant to see Koong Shee. In horror she saw that Ta Jin had brought an engagement gift. His long fingernails were curled around a box of jewels. He looked at her young face with his old eyes and showing her the box, he nodded stiffly to the mandarin. Then the two men went away to plan the wedding.

That night Koong Shee sat weeping at her window. Suddenly, on the moonlit water below she noticed a floating coconut shell. She reached out, and lifting it up she found inside a tiny paper message from Chang.

With great joy she guessed that he must be hiding nearby. She wrote a reply on rice-paper, made it into a sail, and sent the little boat out again onto the water. Her message read, "Gather your fruit when the willow blossom drops onto the water." This, she hoped, would help Chang to guess the date of the wedding.

Bᴜᴛ ɴᴏ ᴡᴏʀᴅ came from Chang. Right up to the wedding night Koong Shee waited for another message. Lanterns were lit and hung amongst the trees, and eventually she was taken into the pagoda where Ta Jin was waiting to marry her, the box of jewels open beside him. But just as the old merchant bent to kiss her hand, Chang, disguised as a boatman, leapt out of the crowd of guests. In a moment of fright Koong Shee snatched up the jewel box, and together the young lovers ran down to the river. The mandarin chased them and for a moment they could be seen on the little hump-backed bridge: Chang leading the way to his boat, Koong Shee carrying the box of jewels, and the old mandarin close behind them brandishing a lantern.

THE TIDE FLOWED AWAY to the East, and carried with it a little boat. Chang steered the silent waters and Koong Shee lay safe inside the cabin. Soon, they were far away.

Their long river journey took them to a poorer part of China where only farming was possible. But they were young and strong and happy to be together. In great secrecy Chang sold the jewels and bought a farm.

At last, Koong Shee and Chang were married. Together they planted apple trees which, under Chang's expert eye, always hung heavy with fruit.

But what of the old mandarin? Every year he sent a new secretary far and wide to search the whole of China for Koong Shee and Chang.

Left alone, he grew old and bitter. The garden became wild without Chang's care, and the fruit and blossoms did not appear on the trees. Soon all the birds of the garden flew away. Only the two turtle doves remained, cooing in their cages where Koong Shee had left them. The birds' calling began to make the mandarin angry, and one day he opened the cages and let them go.

Swift as arrows the birds flew directly east, and at that moment he knew they were flying directly to Koong Shee and Chang.

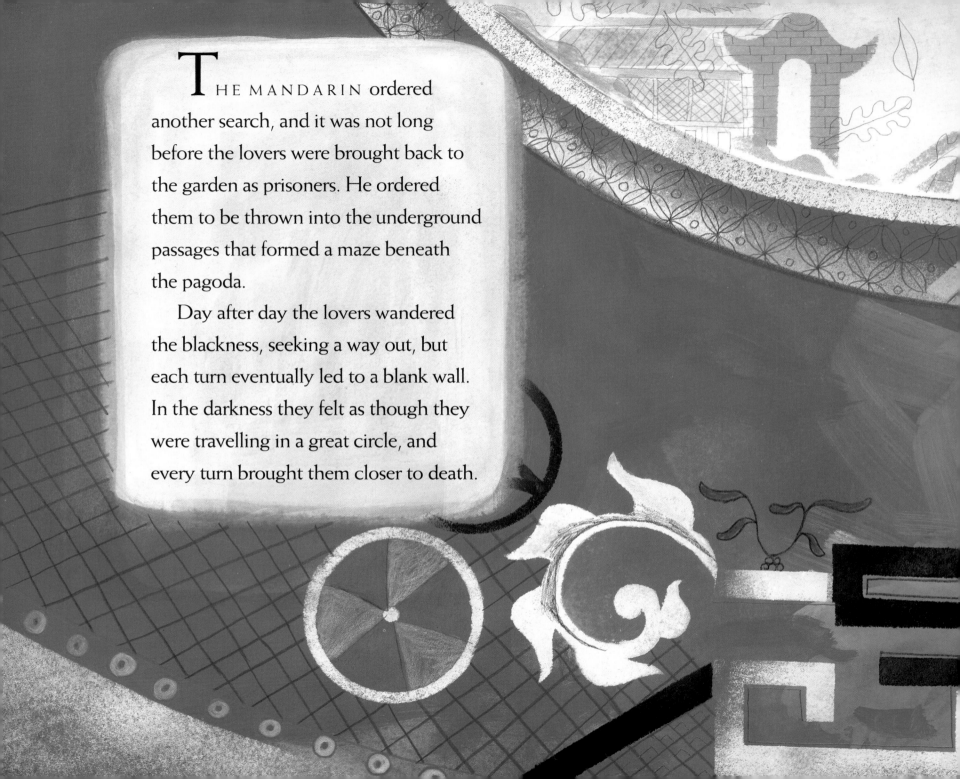

THE MANDARIN ordered
another search, and it was not long
before the lovers were brought back to
the garden as prisoners. He ordered
them to be thrown into the underground
passages that formed a maze beneath
the pagoda.

Day after day the lovers wandered
the blackness, seeking a way out, but
each turn eventually led to a blank wall.
In the darkness they felt as though they
were travelling in a great circle, and
every turn brought them closer to death.

GONE FOREVER were their days in the beautiful apple orchards. Never again would they smell the scent of peonies and camellias at night. Never more would they hear the sound of the birds in the garden, nor the lapping of waves against a boat carried downriver by the tide.

Koong Shee and Chang died together in the great maze underground, and at the same time, the lonely, bitter mandarin died in the pagoda above.

At once, the garden fell silent. The breeze stopped, and with this the leaves on the trees were stilled. The waters of the river ceased their movement as if frozen. The pagoda and its surroundings seemed to be bathed in thin, blue moonlight. . . .

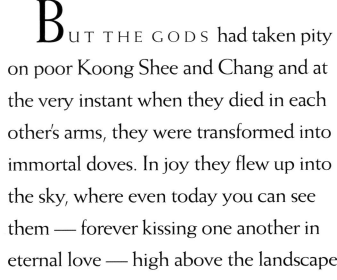

BUT THE GODS had taken pity on poor Koong Shee and Chang and at the very instant when they died in each other's arms, they were transformed into immortal doves. In joy they flew up into the sky, where even today you can see them — forever kissing one another in eternal love — high above the landscape of the willow pattern.

The Story of the Willow Pattern

WHEN I WAS YOUNG my family owned a big jug, decorated with the willow pattern. I must have been curious to know what was going on in the strange blue and white design, but it was not until I became an adult—and I began collecting the broken pieces of blue and white china my wife and I found in our garden—that I started to remember the story I was told as a child.

Each new piece of china provided a glimpse into the mysterious landscape and called back another fragment of the story. Sometimes we found a section of the zig-zag fence, sometimes the maze-like border with its wheels and walls. The more we found the more I became fascinated by the design. We began to buy willow pattern china from antique shops and to research the origins of the design and the stories that were invented to explain it.

Despite its appearance, the

A classic willow pattern plate, manufactured by Spode, circa 1850.

willow pattern is not Chinese in origin. It was first designed and manufactured in England almost 200 years ago. Chinese porcelain was very fashionable at the time and to compete, English manufacturers

copied and adapted many Chinese designs. In about 1795, at the famous Spode pottery works, various Chinese design motifs were combined into a blue and white pattern that would appeal to popular taste. The Spode design was the first true willow pattern.

Willow pattern pottery was very popular from the start and the design was soon applied to a wide range of household items. Because there was no copyright law in nineteenth century England, the Spode design was copied by as many as 100 other firms — often not too well. During the height of its popularity in the 1800s, the willow pattern was copied by manufacturers in other countries around the world. The willow pattern has survived all the changes of fashion for more than two centuries and it is still manufactured and collected today.

No one knows who told the first willow pattern story. There are

many variations and they appear to have started in England in the early 1800s as folk stories, created to fit the different elements of the design. In 1849 a magazine called *The Family Friend* published "The Story of the Willow Pattern Plate." This is the first known printed version of the tragic tale of Koong Shee and Chang, but the author of the story was not named and the origin of the tale remains a mystery. Further evidence of the way the willow design captured the public's imagination is the existence of an old rhyme which describes the pattern:

Two pigeons flying high
Chinese vessel sailing by
Weeping willow hanging o'er
Bridge with three men, if not four
Chinese temples there they stand
Seem to take up all the land

Apple trees with apples on
A pretty fence to end my song.

The story in this book is my own variation, based on the version I was told as a child. I've tried to take the reader on a journey through both the landscape pictured in the design and the border which surrounds it. Looking closely, it seemed to me that the doves were the only things with life in the curiously stiff world beneath them. So the birds became guides for the reader, messengers for the lovers, and in the end, the transformed heroes of the story.

The maze-like border has always fascinated me, so I made it into the great circular dungeon where Koong Shee and Chang spend their last days. The broken fragments on the endpapers of the book are more personal, suggesting

the fragility of china and of my childhood memories.

On the opposite page is a photograph of a classic willow pattern plate. Look closely and you can see all the elements which have fascinated so many people like myself.

Frozen in blue moonlight under shiny glaze, three figures are caught, hurrying across a bridge. Who are they and where are they going? Who is guiding the strange boat as it floats downriver? Who lives in the grand pagoda, which stands behind the zig-zag fence in a beautiful landscape of exotic plants and trees? And what about the doves, who flutter joyfully above the weeping willow? Do they know the secret of what lies below?

A story, it seems, is hidden in the pattern, waiting to be told.

What do *you* think it means?